P9-CMS-603

The Magic Hummingbird

A Hopi Folktale

Collected and Translated by **Ekkehart Malotki**
Narrated by **Michael Lomatuway'ma**
Illustrated by **Michael Lacapa**

KIVA
PUBLISHING, INC.

First Edition

Library of Congress Catalog Card Number 95-080961

Cataloging-in-Publication Data
(Prepared by Quality Books, Inc.)
The Magic hummingbird: a Hopi folktale / collected and translated by
Ekkehart Malotki; narrated by Michael Lomatuway'ma;
illustrated by Michael Lacapa

40 p. cm.
ISBN 1-885772-04-1

1. Hopi Indians--Folklore. 2. Indians of North America--
Arizona--Folklore. 3. Tales--Arizona. I. Malotki, Ekkehart.
II. Lomatuway'ma, Michael. III. Lacapa, Michael, ill.

E99.H7M34 1996   398.2'089'974
QBI95-20578

Designed by Clarissa Pasigan
Printed in Hong Kong

9 8 7 6 5 4 3 2 1

3-96/7.5M/1996

Translator's Note

The objective of this book is two-fold. First, it preserves an authentic folktale in an age when not only is the art of stroytelling sharply declining throughout the world, but whole bodies of oral tradition are vanishing into oblivion. Second, it attempts to fill a perceived void in the availability of quality children's literature based on ethnic sources.

The Magic Hummingbird is an authentic example of Hopi oral literature. Naasiwam Tootsat Pokta, the Hopi version, was related to me in 1984 by Michael Lomatuway'ma. Michael Lacapa's artwork makes the transition from live storyteller to printed page possible. Jointly developing the storyboard with Michael was a delight, and I admire the skill he displayed in capturing the essence of the story in culturally relevant imagery. Thanks are due to my good friend Ken Gary, who greatly improved the readability of the original translation and spent many hours researching the ethnographic literature for descriptions and depictions of the Hopi fertility god Muy'ingwa.

In this age of political correctness, we see too many original stories watered down either to oversimplify or to eliminate any unpleasantness. Several other publishers rejected this story on the grounds that the abandonment of the children at the beginning of the story was"too cruel" and "not fit for children's consumption." The attitude evidenced by these comments betrays an unfortunately common preference for "fakelore" over genuine folklore.

To be sure, famines have occurred in Hopi history, and children may have been abandoned at such life-threatening times. However, the abandonment of the children can also be viewed as a literary device used by the originator of the story, enabling him to narrate it from the viewpoint of the children and thus elicit the listeners' sympathy. Additionally, this device allows him to create the opportunity for the children to become, if not actual heroes, at least instrumental in the survival of Oraibi.

Aliksa'i

Long ago, a great number of people were living at Oraibi, a Hopi village. Each year as it turned summer, the people planted their corn. One year their plants were looking beautiful and healthy, but before they were full grown, they were killed by a frost. All the corn froze, and nothing was left to harvest. The following year the people planted at the usual time. Once again, their plants were nearly mature when they were all killed by frost, leaving nothing to reap. The people tried again the third year, but no sooner did tassels appear on the corn than the plants died from the freezing cold. For a fourth time the people planted. But this time, the young shoots had barely pierced the earth when the frost struck. Once more, all the corn was wiped out.

Life was grim. For four years in a row the people had not harvested any food, and most of their corn stacks and food reserves were gone. Some people had already used up all their supplies. When there was nothing left, they descended from the mesa where Oraibi was located and wandered about in search of something to eat.

Among the people was a couple with two children, a little boy and a little girl. This family, too, had reached the point where all their food was gone. "We'll have to leave to find something to eat," the couple said. "Quite a few people are out of food and have already left. We'll have to do the same, and leave our children behind."

Eventually, all the villagers of Oraibi
abandoned their homes. The only
ones left behind were the little
brother and sister, who had
to rummage through the
trash piles behind the
village to find
something
to eat.

One night when it was already dark, the brother and sister were sitting at home, hungry and miserable. Earlier that day, the little boy, to amuse himself, had picked up the stalk of a sunflower. Now he busied himself with it. Before long he had extracted the soft marrow from the stalk and began molding it in the shape of a hummingbird. When he was done, he handed the bird figure to his little sister. "Here is something for you to play with," he said.

The next morning the boy said to his sister, "Why don't you stay here while I go looking for something to eat. I might come across something somewhere. If I can find even a little bit of food, we won't have to starve for a while yet. But maybe there is nothing out there." With these words he stepped out of the house.

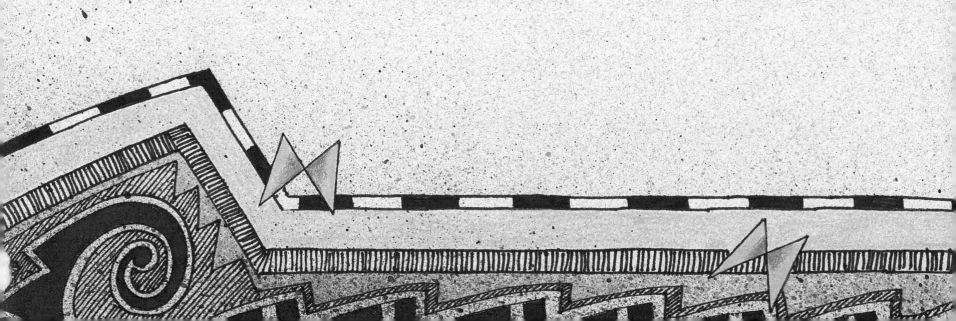

Meanwhile, his little sister just sat there all by herself, playing with the hummingbird figure. This helped her feel content in spite of her loneliness. She was tossing the figure into the air when, suddenly, it came to life! It flew up, circled the room a few times, then darted outside through the hatch in the roof and was gone.

Soon after that, the girl's brother returned, empty-handed. "I don't know what we can eat," he said to this sister. "There is nothing out there. We'll probably have to leave the village and search for food as everyone else has done."

The little girl turned to her brother and said, "Remember the hummingbird you made for me last night? After you left early this morning I started to play with it, and while I was throwing it up in the air, it suddenly came to life and flew away. I don't think we'll ever see it again."

Discouraged, the brother and sister just sat there until evening, when all of a sudden the hummingbird returned. It flew into the house and came to rest in a niche in the wall. The little girl exclaimed, "Our hummingbird is back! This morning it flew away, and now it is back again."

Her brother ran over to the niche, stuck his hand inside and groped around. There was no hummingbird. Instead, to his great surprise, he felt an ear of fresh corn. "Your hummingbird is not here, but here is an ear of fresh corn!" he exclaimed as he pulled it out.

The ear was small, but the two children were overjoyed. Right away they roasted it, broke it in half, and eagerly devoured it. The corn barely diminished their hunger, but at least they had eaten something. They then went to bed.

The following day the brother and sister just sat around. This time the little boy did not bother to go looking for food; there was nothing to be found anyway. That morning while the two were asleep the hummingbird had flown off again, and as they sat there now, it suddenly reappeared. It flew into their house, circled the room a few times, and once more came to rest in the niche in the wall.

The little boy hurried over to the niche and reached in. Much to his amazement, he found another ear of corn inside, slightly larger than the first one. The two children did exactly what they had done before: they roasted the ear, broke it in half and eagerly ate it.

Four times in all the hummingbird brought corn for them, and on the fourth day the boy pulled a very large ear of fresh corn from the niche. The children had no idea where the hummingbird had found the corn, but were grateful. Soon they began to feel slightly less hungry.

The morning after the hummingbird's fourth appearance the little boy reached into the niche again, expecting to find more corn. Instead the hummingbird he had made from stalk marrow was inside, but it was no longer alive. As he inspected it from all sides he muttered, "I wish you were alive so you could search for our parents."

The hummingbird, however, did not move. Turning to his sister, the little boy asked, "How did you make it come alive?"

"This is what I did," she replied, whereupon she took the bird from her brother and threw it up in the air. She did this once, twice, three times, and nothing happened. The fourth time she threw it up, however, it came back to life. Once more it flew up, circled the room a few times, shot out through the hatch in the roof, and was gone.

The hummingbird must have heard the boy's wish, for it left Oraibi and flew in a southwesterly direction. Eventually it reached its destination, a lonely prickly pear cactus. The wretched plant was quite small and bore only a single flower. Despite its poor appearance, the prickly pear stood exactly at Tuuwanasavi, "Earth Center." The humming-bird headed straight for the cactus, and after landing on its flower, opened up a door which led inside.

The inside of the flower resembled a kiva, a Hopi underground chamber. The hummingbird entered, but the room was empty. Flying around, it came to a little hole in the north wall of the kiva. Into that the bird disappeared, only to open another door.

Once more, there was a kiva underneath. The hummingbird looked around, but could not see a soul. There was some green grass sprouting, however, and here and there the blossom of a flower and some corn plants. The bird flew to a tassel and ate some of its pollen. Then it flew into the niche at the far end of the kiva wall and opened it up.

Once again there was a kiva on the other side. This was the third kiva in a row, each one under the other. Upon entering, the hummingbird again found himself alone. In this kiva all sorts of things were growing; there was much more vegetation than in the previous chamber.

Once more the hummingbird flew into a little niche in the north wall, reaching the fourth subterranean dwelling. This kiva was teeming with life and full of flowering fields. All kinds of birds and butterflies happily chased each other around. The hummingbird slipped in and joined the others as they flew about. The other hummingbirds were the first to notice that there was an unfamiliar hummingbird flying around with them.

In the midst of this paradise lived Muy'ingwa, the god of fertility and germination. One of the hummingbirds who also lived there approached the god and said, "A stranger has arrived. He's not one of our flock."

"Is that so? Tell him to come here," Muy'ingwa instructed the hummingbird.

The latter did so and told the visitor to present himself to Muy'ingwa.

The bird landed on the hand of the god. Muy'ingwa looked it over very carefully. Finally he asked, "Who are you? I don't believe you live here, and yet you are flying around with the others."

"That is true," the bird replied. "I'm from Oraibi. A little boy and his sister made me into their pet there."

"Well, you must be here for a reason," Muy'ingwa continued.

"Yes, I am," said the hummingbird.

"Why did you forsake the people of Oraibi? The poor souls have been praying to you, but you have not responded to their prayers. Now they are starving, and all of them except a little boy and his sister had to leave the village. It is on their behalf that I came here. Please, have mercy on them and go out to the upper world again."

"Very well," Muy'ingwa consented. "I will truly do that again."

With this the hummingbird departed, taking with it some of the abundant food for the little boy and girl.

Upon its return, the hummingbird gave the children a whole strand of roasted sweet corn. The ears were large and richly nourishing, and the children devoured them with gusto. Finally, their hunger was truly satisfied.

Then the children turned to the bird. "Remember, you promised to search for our parents. You may or may not find them, but please look for them," the little boy said.

That night the two children went to sleep with their hunger completely gone, but not sure whether the hummingbird would keep his promise. They were still asleep the following morning when the hummingbird set out once again.

After first circling Oraibi, it headed in a northwesterly direction. The hummingbird, of course, is extremely swift, and it was not long before it reached Toho, a place way northwest of Oraibi. There the hummingbird saw many people, among them the children's parents.

The people looked dirty and withered, like skeletons, nothing but skin and bones. Here and there the poor wretches were digging in the ground for wild potatoes that used to grow in that area. Each time one of them was lucky enough to find a little potato, he stuffed it in his mouth just the way it was, gulped it down, and continued foraging for more.

This terrible sight presented itself to the hummingbird as it arrived. It flew by the people, turned and flew past them a second time. Finally a man noticed the bird. "Look, there's a bird flying around," he exclaimed. The man was surprised because he believed there were no other creatures still alive. He thought, "This bird must have discovered life somewhere; otherwise it wouldn't be here now." With that he headed to where the bird had flown.

That very instant the hummingbird appeared, and the man called, "Are you about, stranger?"

The hummingbird heard him, for right away it halted its flight and did what hummingbirds typically do--hovered there. Somehow the bird knew who the man was, and so it replied, "Yes, indeed, and I'm from Oraibi. I just wanted to let you know that your children are still alive." With that the hummingbird shot off again and returned to Oraibi.

The children immediately inquired, "Did you find our parents?"

"Yes, I found them," the hummingbird replied. "I don't know what's going to happen now, but when I found your parents I told them that you are still alive."

In the meantime, Muy'ingwa, the god of germination and fertility, began to keep his promise to the hummingbird. He had agreed to leave his subterranean abode and once again watch over the land above.

He first emerged from the lowermost kiva to the next one above, where he stayed for four days, concentrating his efforts on bringing the crops back to life. As he sat there, clouds began to gather from all directions and slowly move over towards Hopiland. The morning after the fourth day, Muy'ingwa climbed one kiva higher and renewed his prayers for food for the Hopis.

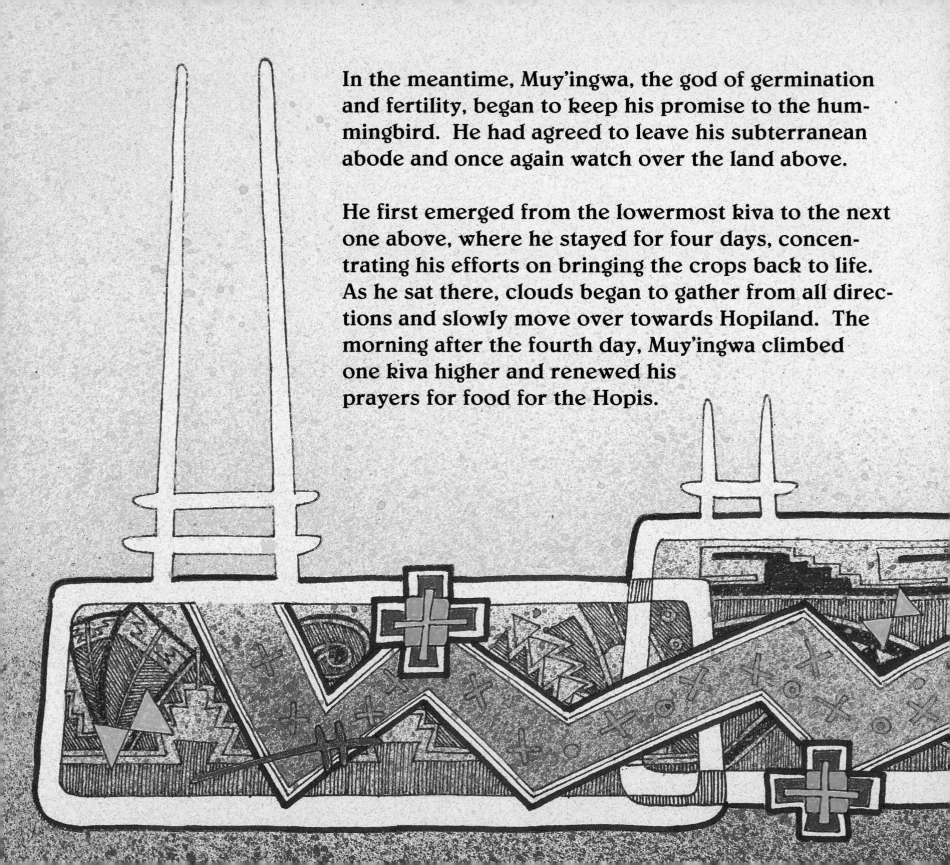

This time, as he engaged in this ritual undertaking, the clouds all came together and released a little bit of moisture, causing a sprinkling rain to fall on the earth. After remaining here four days, the god moved up to the next kiva and spent the same number of days there.

In this kiva he concentrated his prayers on all the plants that make the land look green, especially on the crops.

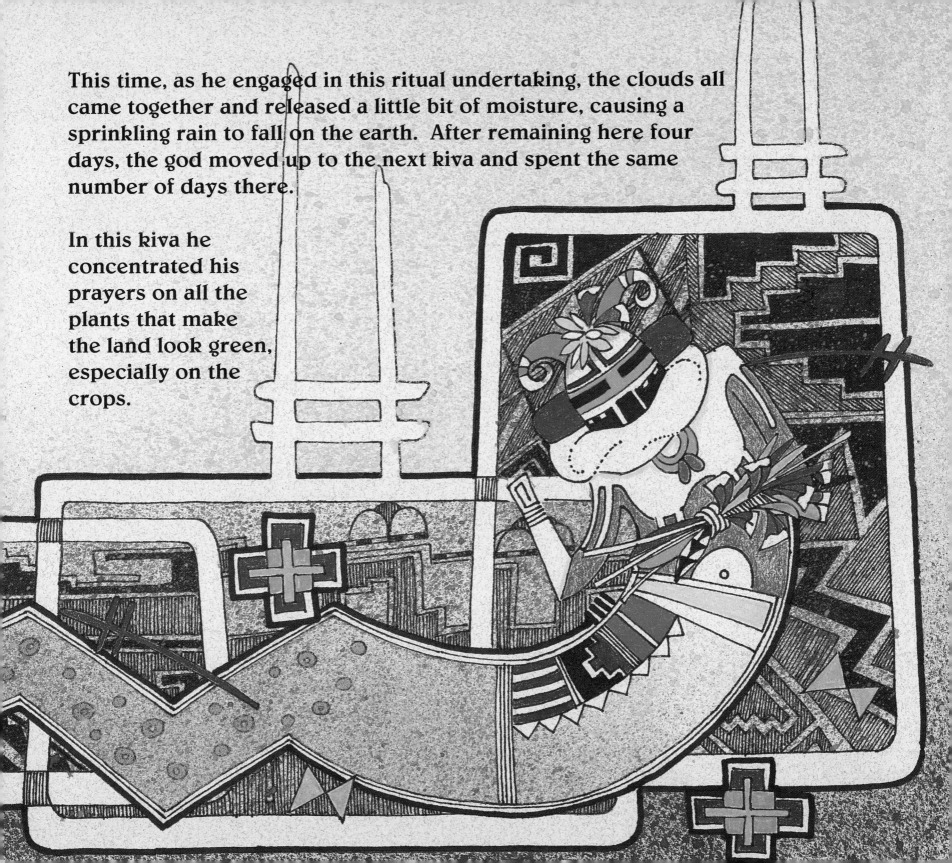

Now the clouds really showed that they meant business to dump all their rain on the ground. For four days and four nights it rained like this. When the rain finally stopped, all the check dams and ponds were filled to the brim with water. As far as the eye could see, the land was shining with puddles. The earth was saturated through and through with moisture, and every corner of the land was beginning to look green again. All the plants which normally bear flowers bloomed, and life once more returned to what it had been before.

Only then did Muy'ingwa make his exit to the earth's surface. As he looked about, the world was beautiful again.

In the north, the people now also noticed the change that had come over the land. Clearly it had rained all the way from where they were to Oraibi. "It must have rained at our village too," they said, and began to move back to Oraibi. When they arrived there, everything was coming back to life again, and the plain below Oraibi was one great green expanse.

So it was in this manner that a hummingbird, who at first had not even been a living creature, succeeded in persuading Muy'ingwa, this most powerful deity, to help the Oraibi people. After that Muy'ingwa never again retreated so deeply underground.

Thus Oraibi recovered, thanks to the two children who fashioned a hummingbird and made it come alive; thanks also to the hummingbird who pitied the children, and on their behalf pleaded with Muy'ingwa at Earth Center to restore life. I guess the people are still living there at Oraibi.

And here the story ends.

About the Translator

Ekkehart Malotki, Ph.D., is a professor of languages at Northern Arizona University, where he teaches German, Hopi and Latin. His work as a philologist and ethnolinguist concentrates on the preservation of Hopi language and culture and the recording and analysis of rock art in Northern Arizona. In addition to bilingual works involving Hopi semantics and Hopi oral literature, he has published a children's book, The Mouse Couple, and co-authored the rock art work Tapamveni: The Rock Art Galleries of Petrified Forest and Beyond. He also contributed Hopi titles for Godfrey Reggio's movies Koyaanisqatsi and Powaqqatsi. Since 1986 he has been working with a team from the University of Arizona on the comprehensive Hopi Dictionary Project.

About the Illustrator

Michael Lacapa is an artist, author and educator. He earned his B.A. in art education at Arizona State University, and has completed graduate work in painting and printmaking at Northern Arizona University. Of Apache, Tewa and Hopi descent, he works with school-age children in and around the White Mountain Apache Reservation, and lives with his wife and three children in Taylor, Arizona. The Magic Hummingbird is Michael's fifth illustrated children's book. He started in 1988 with The Mouse Couple, authored and illustrated The Flute Player (1990) and Antelope Woman (1992), and co-authored (with his wife Kathleen) and illustrated Less Than Half, More Than Whole (1994).